MR. KATAPAT'S
Incredible Adventures

BARROUX

VIKING

This is our hero,
Mr. Katapat.

He may look like an ordinary man,

but really he is a great adventurer.

Every day, Mr. Katapat heads to the library.

That's right, the library.

It's where all the excitement begins.

Now you know Mr. Katapat's secret—

books are his passport to adventure!

Which book will he choose today?

Some days he is a fortune hunter, exploring the jungle in search of an ancient pygmy temple.

Other days, he travels back in time

to meet the giants of history!

Nice thinking cap, Mr. Lincoln.

And sometimes he's Sheriff Katapat,

bringing justice to the Wild West.

Hold your horses!

What's that on the horizon?

Avast, ye hearties!

Pirates have boarded Captain Katapat's ship!

Can he fight them off,

or will he walk the plank?

If only his real life were as exciting.

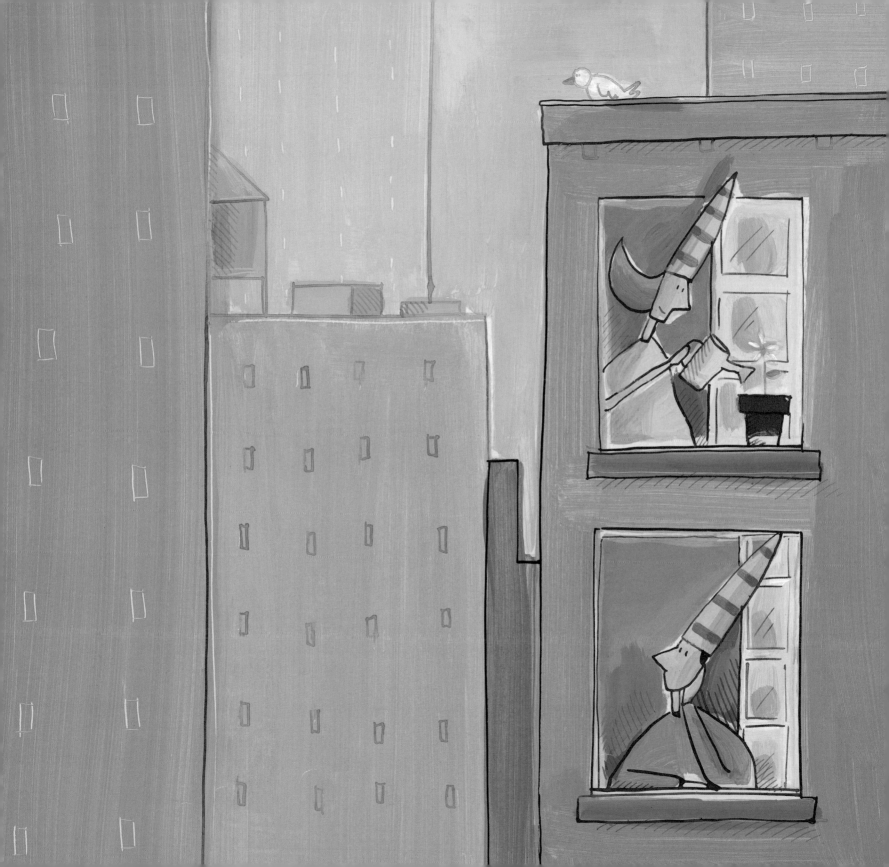

Real life can't compare to the time he faced the greatest kung fu master in all of China.

When he's Sir Katapat,
slaying dragons and rescuing
princesses are all in a day's work.

No mystery is too great for Detective Katapat.

Aha! the missing clue—another case closed!

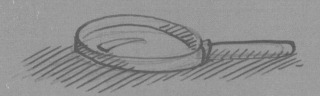

Mornings at the South Pole with the penguins,

afternoons exploring the great pyramids...

... Mr. Katapat never knows
when adventure will strike next!

What's this?

Mr. Katapat has stumbled into a real life adventure.

You see, he has never read this book.

It looks like a love story. . . .

That is how Mr. Katapat

met Mrs. Katapat.

These days, they can be found

turning the pages of a new book.

But that's another story.

for my mother

VIKING

Published by Penguin Group

Penguin Young Readers Group, 345 Hudson Street, New York, New York 10014, U.S.A.

Penguin Books Ltd, 80 Strand, London WC2R 0RL, England

Penguin Books Australia Ltd, 250 Camberwell Road, Camberwell, Victoria 3124, Australia

Penguin Books Canada Ltd, 10 Alcorn Avenue, Toronto, Ontario, Canada M4V 3B2

Penguin Group (NZ), cnr Airborne and Rosedale Roads, Albany, Auckland 1310, New Zealand

First published in 2004 by Viking, a division of Penguin Young Readers Group

1 3 5 7 9 10 8 6 4 2

LIBRARY OF CONGRESS CATALOGING-IN-PUBLICATION DATA

Barroux, Stephane.

Mr. Katapat's incredible adventures / Barroux.

p. cm.

Summary: Each day, an ordinary man becomes a great adventurer when he goes to the library

and reads about the Wild West, pirates, or a visit to the pyramids.

ISBN 0-670-05916-1 (hardcover)

[1. Books and reading—Fiction. 2. Adventure and adventurers—Fiction.] I. Title.

PZ7.B275675Mr 2004

[E]—dc22

2004004084

Manufactured in China

Book design by Jim Hoover

Set in Vendetta Medium